What Could Be Keeping Santa?

What Could Be

Keeping Santa?

By Marilyn Janovitz

North-South Books · *New York* · *London*

Reindeer standing in a row,

Shadows falling on the snow

The sleigh is packed, all set to go!
What could be keeping Santa?

The Christmas tree is straight and tall,

Mistletoe's hanging in a ball,

And holly decorates the hall.
What could be keeping Santa?

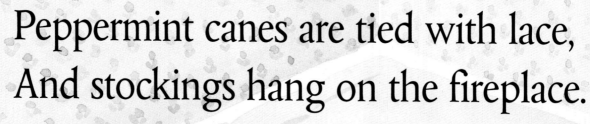

Peppermint canes are tied with lace,
And stockings hang on the fireplace.

Tick-tock, tick-tock, no time to waste!
What could be keeping Santa?

Did he forget this special date?

Why would he make eight reindeer wait?

He's never, ever been so late.

What could be keeping Santa?

Think of the children, how sad they'll be
On Christmas morning if they don't see
Presents waiting under the tree.
What could be keeping Santa?

At Santa's door they gave a knock,
Then called, "You're late! Look at the clock!"

They waited. Would the door unlock?

What could be keeping Santa?

"My dear deer friends, you'll have to wait.
You're one day early—check the date!
On Christmas Eve we won't be late....

"Nothing would *ever* keep Santa!"

To Marc and Julie

Published in the United States by North-South Books Inc., New York.
Published simultaneously in Great Britain, Canada, Australia, and
New Zealand in 1997 by North-South Books, an imprint of
Nord-Süd Verlag AG, Gossau Zürich, Switzerland.

Library of Congress Cataloging-in-Publication Data is available.
A CIP catalogue record for this book is available from The British Library.

The artwork consists of colored pencil and watercolors.
Designed by Marc Cheshire

ISBN 1-55858-819-1 (trade binding)
1 3 5 7 9 TB10 8 6 4 2
ISBN 1-55858-820-5 (library binding)
1 3 5 7 9 LB 10 8 6 4 2
Printed in Belgium

For more information about our books, and the authors and artists
who create them, visit our web site: http://www.northsouth.com